Love

Written by Willie Deane

Illustrated by Miša Jovanović

S0-APP-336

Love

Copyright © 2019 by Willie Deane. All rights reserved.

No rights claimed for public domain material, all rights reserved. No parts of this publication may be reproduced, stored in any retrieval system, or transmitted in any form or by any means, electronic, mechanical, recording, or otherwise, without the prior written permission of the author. Violations may be subject to civil or criminal penalties.

Library of Congress Control Number: 2018968281

ISBN:
978-1-63308-467-4 (hardback)
978-1-63308-468-1 (paperback)
978-1-63308-469-8 (ebook)

Illustrated by Miša Jovanović

CHALFANT ECKERT
PUBLISHING

1028 S Bishop Avenue, Dept. 178
Rolla, MO 65401

Printed in United States of America

Love

Written by Willie Deane

Illustrated by Miša Jovanović

CHALFANT ECKERT

PUBLISHING

This book belongs to

_____

DEDICATION

To my daughters who inspire me
to be a better father, to my wife who inspires
me to be a better husband, to my parents who
inspire me to educate myself continually,
and to the city of Schenectady who
inspired me to be the man I am.
Thank you!

"Sara wake up! Wake up! Wake up baby, we overslept! You have to hurry up and get dressed before you are late for school."

As I lie in my bed, exhausted from staying up too late the night before, my mother's words sounded like she was speaking to me from underwater.

Once she yanked off my covers, the lack of warmth that I was enjoying while underneath my blankets was no more, and the sudden drop in temperature didn't feel as pleasant. As soon as the winter air that had seeped through my window during the night touched my skin, the chill woke me from my daze.

"I'm awake, Mom," I answered.

"Okay, good," said Mother.

"Now let's hurry up and get dressed. I already have your breakfast on the table waiting for you, Sara."

I quickly threw some clothes on before rushing downstairs. As I approached the final two steps, I could already smell the mouth-watering aroma.

My favorite – pancakes with butter, maple syrup, and a glass of orange juice; yummy!

My mother was always on me about eating a good breakfast. She believed breakfast was the most important meal of the day and just the right thing to help the body produce enough energy to tackle what the day has planned for us.

After breakfast, I brushed my teeth and was lucky to make the bus.

The bus driver was running a little late too, which I thought was funny. In any case, I was still happy my mother didn't have to go out of her way to take me to school because then she would have been late for work. But I knew she would have driven me if necessary.

Right before boarding the bus, my mother gave me a hug, a kiss on my forehead, and told me she loved me.

I responded by telling her, "I love you too, Mom," as I hurried to get to my seat.

From as far back as I can remember, this was our routine, but for some reason, today the word **Love** stuck with me.

Love, I thought. *What is this word? What does it even mean? Why do my parents always tell me that they love me?*

All through school, I had this word *love* on my brain. When the final bell rang marking the end of school, I jumped up from my desk, grabbed my books, and hurried to my locker.

After putting on my hat, scarf, and coat, I ran to the bus. I couldn't get home fast enough. I just had to ask my mother what this love word actually meant, and why there isn't a day that goes by that she or my father doesn't say it to me.

I say love too. I always have. It is what my parents say to me, so how else am I to respond? Anyway, it was time to get down to the bottom of what love means.

I hopped off the bus and sprinted into my parents' arms. They work during the week but always make sure that they are there to greet me when I come home from school.

"Mommy and Daddy," I said, "What is…"

I was quickly interrupted by my parents as they asked in unison, "How was your day baby? Did you have a good day at school? What did you learn today?"

My dad always asked me what I learned. He always told me that a day that goes by without learning something new is a day wasted.

Another one of his favorite quotes was, "Don't waste time Sara, because time wasted can never be recovered."

As I answered all the questions that they bounced off me, one thing led to another, and before I knew it, I was at my desk doing my homework.

After finishing my homework,
we ate dinner together as a
family (like we always do).
I was so hungry from the
long day that I completely
forgot about asking my
parents about this
mysterious word
called *love*.

Besides, my parents also don't like for me to talk with food in my mouth. They said that it wasn't polite or proper etiquette to do such, and as hungry as I was, I don't think there was a time during dinner that I didn't have food in my mouth until I was stuffed.

Mother cleared the table and asked me politely to go upstairs, wash up, and get ready for bed.

Once she and my father finished cleaning and putting the food away, they would be up there shortly to tuck me in for the night.

I did what I was told. I brushed my teeth, put my dirty clothes in the hamper, took a shower, and put on my pajamas before climbing into bed.

After about ten minutes, my parents entered my room to tuck me in. This was my chance, and I took it. I asked immediately before they could reach my bed.

"Mommy and Daddy," I said.

"Yes baby," my parents replied.

"What is *Love*?" I asked.

My father led, "Well Sara, Love is probably one of the most powerful forms of expression in the world."

"What does that mean, Daddy?" I asked.

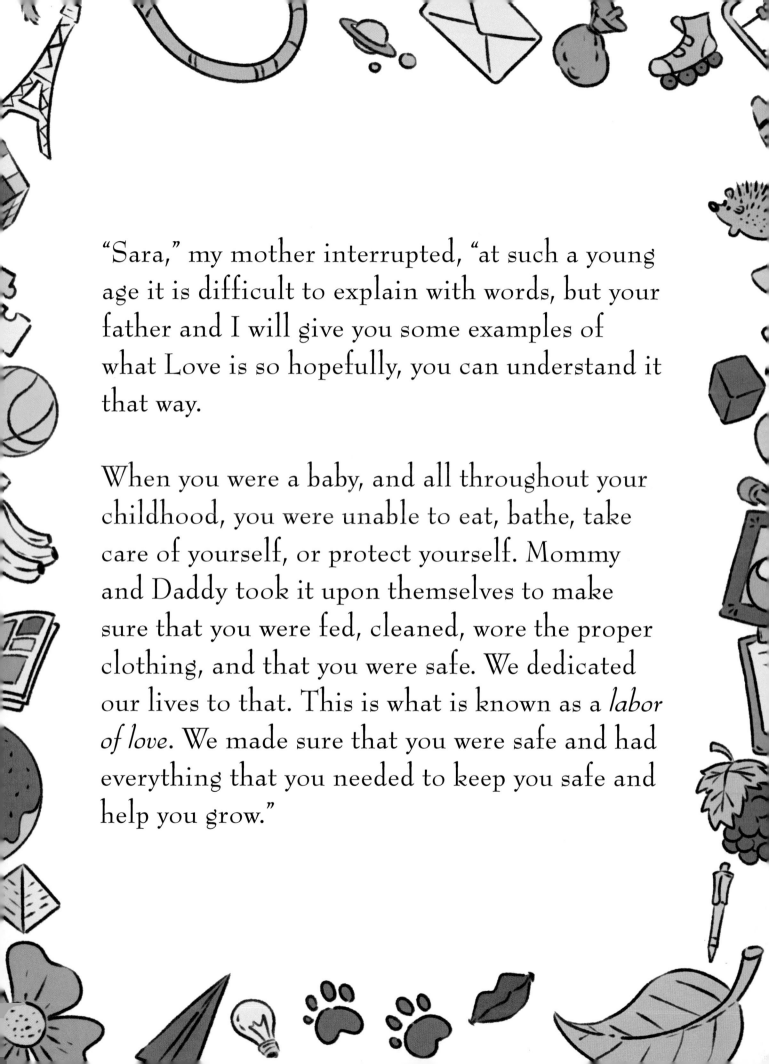

"Sara," my mother interrupted, "at such a young age it is difficult to explain with words, but your father and I will give you some examples of what Love is so hopefully, you can understand it that way.

When you were a baby, and all throughout your childhood, you were unable to eat, bathe, take care of yourself, or protect yourself. Mommy and Daddy took it upon themselves to make sure that you were fed, cleaned, wore the proper clothing, and that you were safe. We dedicated our lives to that. This is what is known as a *labor of love*. We made sure that you were safe and had everything that you needed to keep you safe and help you grow."

Daddy asked, "Sara, can you think of any other ways of expressing or showing love?"

A silence fell upon the room.

After some time passed, I guessed, "A hug and a kiss?"

"That's what you and Mommy do to me every day."

"That's right Sara! That would be a perfect example of expressing love in the form of a touch. You are doing great," my parents said.

Mommy asked, "Can you think of any more expressions of love?"

"Um, no Mommy. I just know that we say *I love you* to each other all the time."

"Great Sara!"

"What?" I said with a confused look on my face.

"What did I say?"

"Nothing wrong baby, you just gave us another great example of a way of showing or expressing love, "said Mother.

"How is that?" I asked?

Mommy answered, "When we tell each other that we love each other, we are expressing our love in the form of words."

"Keep it going, baby girl!" Daddy said in his exciting and most encouraging voice.

I ordered, "Tell me, Daddy! I can't think of any more."

"Ok then, let me give you a hint," said Daddy. "What did we do yesterday?"

No less than a second passed before I yelled, "We went to the park!"

"Yes, baby, we did! Soooooo," Daddy said.

"What?" I said. "I don't get it Daddy."

"Let's take yesterday, for example," said Daddy. "We went to the park, we watched a movie at home, and that evening, we sat on the couch and read books together. What we were doing in all those examples was spending quality time together, which can be another way of showing that you love someone."

"It is getting late Sara, so Mommy and I will tell you the last two examples that we know as ways of expressing and showing love. One example," Daddy said, "is by our actions. When we go out of our way to be nice to someone, that can be seen as an action of love."

I interrupted, "Like when you leave work early sometimes to meet me coming off the bus after school?"

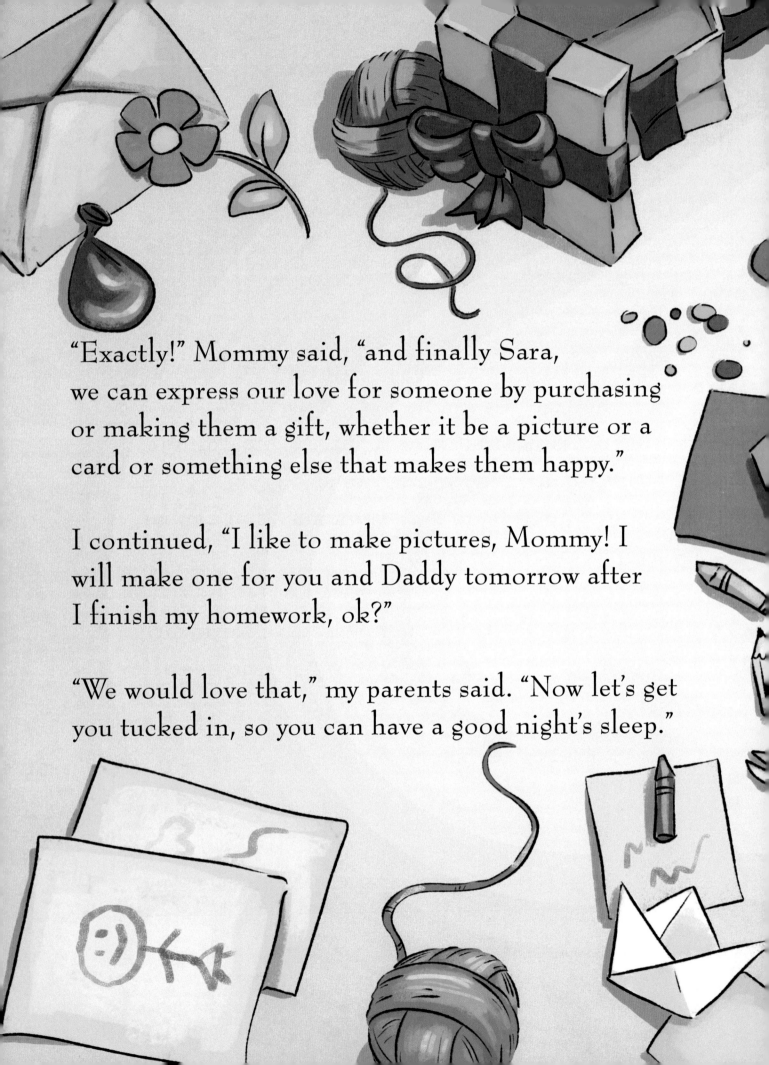

"Exactly!" Mommy said, "and finally Sara, we can express our love for someone by purchasing or making them a gift, whether it be a picture or a card or something else that makes them happy."

I continued, "I like to make pictures, Mommy! I will make one for you and Daddy tomorrow after I finish my homework, ok?"

"We would love that," my parents said. "Now let's get you tucked in, so you can have a good night's sleep."

"Mommy and Daddy …"

"Yes, baby?" they said waiting for my answer.

"I wish everyone would love each other. If everyone did those things that we spoke about, then the world would be a much better place."

"You are absolutely right, Sara. We couldn't agree with you more!"

Both my mother and father bent down to kiss me gently on my forehead before tucking me in nice and tight. As they walked towards my door to exit, they turned off my light.

My room was almost completely dark except for the light rays that crept in my bedroom from the hallway.

Just as my father was getting ready to close the door, I blurted out "Mommy and Daddy,"

"Yes, Sara?" they answered.

"I love you!" I said.

Right before they closed the door and my room turned pitch black, my parents both responded, "We love you too, Sara."

As I lay warm and comfortable in my bed and right before falling to sleep, I mumbled to myself, "Mmmm, love."

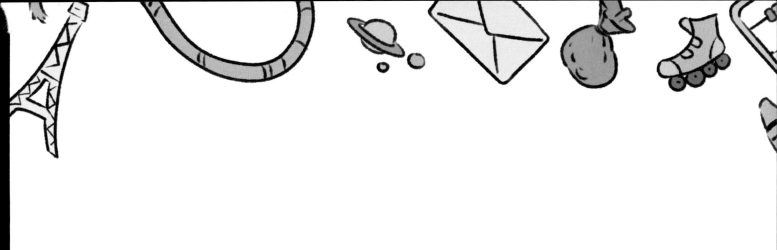

Made in the USA
Middletown, DE
19 June 2022

67233767R00031